THE TERROR TOAD

By Jean Waricha

A PARACHUTE PRESS BOOK

GROSSET & DUNLAP • NEW YORK

A PARACHUTE PRESS BOOK
Parachute Press, Inc.
156 Fifth Avenue
New York, NY 10010

Published by Grosset & Dunlap, Inc., a member of The Putnam &
Grosset Group, New York. GROSSET & DUNLAP is a trademark of
Grosset & Dunlap, Inc. Published simultaneously in Canada.

Creative Consultant: Cheryl Saban.

With special thanks to Cheryl Saban, Sheila Dennen, Debi Young, and
Sherry Stack.

Printed in the U.S.A.
May 1994
ISBN: 0-448-40831-7
C D E F G H I J

The Battle Begins

Long ago, Good and Evil met in a great battle. The wizard Zordon led the forces of Good. He fought against Rita Repulsa, who wanted to rule the universe with her forces of Evil.

Both sides fought hard, but the war ended in a tie. So Zordon and

1

Rita made a deal. They would both flip coins to decide who was the winner. Whoever made the best three tosses out of five would win. The loser would be locked away forever.

Of course, Zordon did not want to risk the safety of the universe on five coins—unless they were magic coins! So with his five special coins, Zordon won the coin toss. But Rita had one last trick up her sleeve. Before she was locked away, she trapped Zordon in another dimension. Now he must stay inside a column of green light at his command center forever and ever.

Rita and her wicked friends were dropped into an intergalactic prison and flung through space. They crashed into a tiny moon of a faraway planet. After ten thousand years, space travelers found the prison and opened it. Rita and her servants, Baboo, Squatt, Goldar, and Finster, were free!

Rita hadn't changed one bit in ten thousand years. She began planning to take over the universe again. And she saw her first target in the sky above—Earth!

When Zordon heard of Rita's escape, he put his master plan into action. He called Alpha 5, the robot running his command center on Earth. "Teleport to us five of the wildest, most willful humans in the area," he commanded.

"No!" Alpha 5 said. "Not... teenagers!"

But Alpha 5 did as he was told, and teleported five teenagers to the command center.

"Earth is under attack by the evil Rita Repulsa," Zordon explained to the teenagers. "I have chosen you to battle her and save the planet. Each of you will receive great powers drawn from the spirits of the dinosaurs."

Zordon gave each teenager a

belt with a magic coin—a Power Morpher! "When you are in danger, raise your Power Morpher to the sky," Zordon instructed. "Then call out the name of your dinosaur and you will morph into a mighty fighter—a Power Ranger!

"Jason, you will be the Red Ranger, with the power of the great tyrannosaurus," Zordon explained. "Trini will be the Yellow Ranger, with the force of the saber-toothed tiger. Zack will be the Black Ranger, with the power of the mastodon. Kimberly will be the Pink Ranger, with pterodactyl power. And Billy will be the Blue Ranger, backed by the power of the triceratops."

For big problems, the Power Rangers could call upon Dinozords—giant robots they piloted into battle. And if things got really tough, the Dinozords could combine together to make a super-robot—a mighty Megazord!

Power Rangers, dinosaur spirits, and robots—together, these incredible forces would protect the Earth.

But the teenagers had to follow Zordon's three rules:

1. Never use your powers for selfish reasons.

2. Never make a fight worse—unless Rita forces you.

3. Always keep your identities secret. No one must ever find out that you are a Mighty Morphin Power Ranger!

CHAPTER 1

Early Friday morning, the Angel Grove Youth Center was empty except for five teenagers— Jason, Zack, Billy, Trini, and Kimberly. They were best friends. But the five shared more than friendship. Trini, Kimberly, Jason, Zack, and Billy had superpowers.

Whenever the Earth was attacked by evil forces, the five teenagers turned into the Mighty Morphin Power Rangers. Their job: to protect the planet!

Battling Evil was far from their minds today. They were getting ready to practice for the upcoming volleyball game. Zack, Jason, and Trini collected the equipment and headed for the volleyball court. Kimberly and Billy stayed behind in the youth center kitchen. Kimberly was mixing up something she called her "secret weapon" as Billy watched, his blue eyes growing wider and wider behind his glasses. "Can I talk to you about something?" he asked.

"Sure, Billy," Kimberly said, adding the final ingredient. She had on pink shorts and a pink tank top. A pink headband held her brown bangs back. In front of her on the countertop were several half-squeezed oranges and lemons, bottles of vitamins, containers of powdered milk, and packets of sugar.

"What are you doing?" asked Billy. He had done hundreds of science experiments, but had never seen anything like this one.

"I'm making a Power Drink for us," Kimberly said. "It will give us extra energy so we can win the volleyball game."

"I didn't know you were so interested in cooking," Billy said. "I thought your specialty was shopping."

"Very funny," said Kimberly. "This is serious. This drink is going to charge your batteries."

Kimberly finished making the drink, and Billy helped her clean the counter. He read the labels on the ingredients she used.

"Actually, Kimberly," he said, "this drink has all the right chemical compositions to increase our energy levels...."

Kimberly grinned. Billy was

really, really smart, but some-
times he sounded like a teacher.
"Let's get to practice," she said.

On the way to the court, Billy
walked very slowly. "We're going
to be late," Kimberly said. "Don't
you want to play?"

"Well, that's what I wanted to
talk to you about. I'm a little ner-
vous about the volleyball game,"
said Billy. "I'm not that good a
player. I don't want to mess up
the game for everyone else."

Kimberly put her arm around
his shoulders. "Billy, we're a
team, and we stick together!
Besides, my Power Drink will turn
you into a different person."

* * *

Miles and miles away from Earth, Rita Repulsa sat on the balcony of her fortress on the moon. Her favorite pastime was spying on the Power Rangers. Once she got them out of the way, she could destroy their planet. Now she was listening to Billy and Kimberly as they walked to the volleyball court.

Baboo stood next to her. He was Rita's chief chemist, potion maker, and nail polisher. He held a bottle of black nail polish in his hand.

"Stand still, you twit," shouted Rita. She dipped her nail brush into the bottle. "What do you think of this color? Do you think it should be darker?"

Baboo looked at Rita's long, pointed nails. "It's perfect for you," he answered. "Black is your color. It matches your eyes."

"Those stupid teenagers," Rita grumbled as she dipped the nail brush into the bottle once again. "What do they know about Power Drinks?" Then she jumped from her chair and screamed, "I've got it! I know how to destroy the Power Rangers!

"Come, Baboo," she said, dragging him by the ear. "We've got work to do."

CHAPTER 2

On the Angel Grove volleyball court, Trini, Zack, and Jason were warming up. "Nice hit!" Jason shouted as Trini spiked the volleyball over the net, her long black hair flying behind her. Trini's height helped to make her a good player.

Zack lunged and bumped the ball back. "Oh no," he groaned. He had hit it right to Jason. Jason slammed the ball back across the net just as Billy and Kimberly entered the volleyball court.

"Hi guys!" Kimberly yelled, waving to Jason, Zack, and Trini. "Billy and I are ready to play, but I'd better warn you that we have a secret weapon."

Just then, Bulk and Skull, Angel Grove's biggest troublemakers, walked onto the volleyball court. Bulk looked ridiculous, as usual. He wore white cutoff jeans and high green socks. An orange sweatband was wrapped around his head. And under his black leather jacket, he wore a purple tie-dyed shirt. Skull, his skinny, dark-haired pal, was dressed all in black.

"Is this your secret weapon?" asked Zack, pointing to Bulk and Skull. "One look at them and the other team will laugh until they drop!"

"This court is reserved for our practice," Trini told Bulk. "You'll have to leave."

"Bulk is so good that people think he should play professional volleyball," Skull said. "Show them your moves, Bulk."

"This ought to be really good,"

Jason said with a grin.

Skull went to one side of the net and served the ball to Bulk, but the ball fell short. Bulk charged the net and ran right into it. The net gave under his weight, then shot him back across the court.

"This way," said Skull, leading a very dizzy Bulk off the court.

"Hey, Bulk. I've never seen moves like yours!" Zack called after them.

As soon as they were gone, the Power Rangers played a few practice games.

"Good shot, Billy!" Jason shouted as Billy returned Trini's serve.

"Hey guys, let's take a break," Kimberly suggested after their third game.

She headed to the bench at the edge of the court. She picked up her thermos and said, "Now it's time for my homemade Power Drink! Who's going to be the first to try it?"

No one answered.

"Come on, Billy," Kimberly pouted. "How about you?"

While Kimberly tried to convince Billy to take a sip of her drink, someone else was making a special Power Drink, too—someone on the moon.

* * *

Rita and Baboo huddled in Baboo's lab. The room was dark and damp. Cages full of strange animals lined one side of the wall, and jars of pickled insects lined another. A terrible foul odor filled the air.

"Oh, I just love the smell of this room," said Rita. "You must try to bottle it for me. But first we have to work on *my* Power Drink—my hate potion! Now!"

"Calm yourself, Your Awfulness," said Baboo. "I have just the right recipe. One drop of this potion will turn those goody-goody teenagers into the worst kids in Angel Grove. Then they'll turn on each other and destroy themselves."

"And I'll be free to destroy the Earth!" Rita cackled.

Baboo rushed around the lab. He collected all sorts of odd ingredients. There were bottles of foaming green liquid, cans of hundred-year-old anchovies, bottles of moldy ketchup, jars of mosquito wings, and a can of axle grease.

Baboo mixed everything together in a large beaker, then zapped it in the microwave on high for one minute.

Rita paced back and forth as he worked, scratching at the pointy cones of her hat with her black nails. "Hurry up with that potion, you stupid twit. If we are going to fix the Power Rangers' drinks we need that potion this minute!" Then she screamed for Finster.

"You called, my Empress of Evil?" Finster answered, rushing into the room.

"You must send the Putty Patrol to lure the Power Rangers away from the thermos at once. Or they'll drink that silly girl's Power Drink before we can get to it. We've got to hurry!"

As Rita finished bellowing, the microwave beeped. Glowing red smoke billowed out the door.

"It's done!" cried Baboo.

He took an eyedropper and squeezed up a small amount of the red liquid. "I'll need only one drop," he said. "One drop and the Power Rangers will be destroyed!"

Back in Angel Grove,
Kimberly poured two cups of the
Power Drink—one for herself and
one for Billy.

"Billy, are you really going to
drink that stuff?" asked Zack.

"Certainly," said Billy. "But not
just yet. Look!" He pointed over

Zack's head.

"The Putty Patrollers!" Trini cried.

"Well, well, well," said Jason, his brown eyes flashing. "Look who wants to play volleyball."

Rita's mindless clay creatures somersaulted onto the volleyball court and attacked the Power Rangers, splitting them up. There were two Putties to every Power Ranger.

The Power Rangers used all their karate skill and acrobatic training to hold off the attacking Putties. They were much too busy to notice Baboo's arrival.

Baboo hid under the bench

where Kimberly had placed the drinks. He reached into his pocket and took out the small bottle of red liquid. He placed a drop of the potion in each cup. Then he unscrewed the top of the thermos and dumped the rest of the potion into it.

Baboo slowly counted to four. On the count of four, the liquid inside the cups and thermos glowed red. "It's all set, Your Badness," he whispered, looking toward the moon. "Please bring us home."

In a flash, Baboo and the Putties were gone.

"I wonder what Rita's up to this

time," said Zack as he brushed off his green and black sweats.

"I wish we knew," said Billy. He picked up one of the drinks on the bench. "Boy, I really need this. Fighting always makes me thirsty."

"Me, too," said Kimberly, reaching for the other cup.

Billy and Kimberly each took a big sip. As they swallowed their drinks, their faces turned bright red and their bodies began to shake. Kimberly sat down hard on the bench. She knocked over the thermos bottle. It went crashing to the ground, and broke into hundreds of pieces.

"Are you guys all right?" asked Trini, her dark eyes full of concern.

But Billy didn't answer.

Something is wrong, Trini thought. Something is terribly wrong.

CHAPTER 4

"Are you okay, Billy?" asked Jason as he and Zack ran over to the group. "Are you sick?"

"Yeah, I'm sick all right," Billy finally replied, sneering. "Sick of the sight of you three nerds."

"Right on, baby," Kimberly said, hanging onto Billy's arm. She gave Jason a cold stare.

Zack, Jason, and Trini looked at each other. Now they *knew* something was wrong.

"Hey, man," Jason said, "you're not yourselves. Let us help you."

"Okay," said Billy, "you can help us by not using up our air. Go take a walk in traffic."

Kimberly started to giggle. Billy put his arm around her and said, "Let's split." Then the two of them strolled away, leaving their stunned friends behind.

The next day at school, Jason, Zack, and Trini looked for Billy and Kimberly.

The Putties interrupt the Power Ranger volleyball game, but Kimberly shows them some manners!

Trini takes a fighting position.

Zack and Jason dodge a Putty attack.

Billy and Kimberly have turned punk under Rita's spell!

"Is there any way to bring them back to normal?" Jason asks Zordon.

"Aye-yi-yi-yi! I have to get Billy and Kimberly the cure!" says Alpha.

Zack, Jason, and Trini morph to fight Rita's newest monster, the Terror Toad.

The Power Rangers appear in Angel Grove.

**Billy listens as Zordon explains how to
defeat the toad.**

The Power Rangers have stopped Rita's evil plans again!

They found Billy in the school cafeteria talking to a younger boy who was wearing a baseball hat. Billy had backed the boy against a wall.

"Is that Billy?" said Trini in disbelief. "What did he do to himself?" In place of his normally neat pants and shoes, Billy was wearing heavy black boots and jeans ripped at the knees. A red bandanna was tied around his head.

Zack, Trini, and Jason edged closer so they could hear what Billy was saying. "Where's your lunch money, kid? Hand it over."

"No way," said the younger student. "No way!"

Billy knocked the boy's hat off his head and laughed. The younger student grabbed his hat from the floor and ran off. Billy started after him, but stopped when he spotted Jason, Zack, and Trini.

"What are you geeks looking at?" he said.

"Yeah, take a picture, it lasts longer," said Kimberly, who came up beside Billy.

"Hey, Kimberly," said Billy, "that's a good one." Then Billy and Kimberly slapped hands.

"Billy, why did you knock that boy's hat off?" Trini asked.

Billy was about to answer when Kimberly chimed in. "Don't you guys have anything better to do than to spy on Billy?"

That's when Trini noticed Kimberly's clothes.

"Kimberly, where did you get those clothes?" Trini asked.

Kimberly twirled around in front of Trini, showing off her new outfit. She wore a short leather skirt with a purple blouse held together with safety pins—not at all like the leggings and matching T-shirts she usually wore.

"Why, don't you like it?" Kimberly said. "Come on, Billy, let's get out of here. I don't want anyone to see me with these dweebs."

"Wait," Trini called, reaching out for Kimberly's hand.

But Kimberly pushed it away and shouted, "Bug off!" Then she and Billy left.

Trini's eyes widened and she looked as if she was about to cry. "We've got to do something about Billy and Kimberly," she said. "We're going to lose our best friends."

"I think you're right," Jason agreed. "But we're going to need help. Let's get to Zordon—fast!"

CHAPTER 5

"**We did it!** We did it!" Rita yelled, watching Billy and Kimberly through her telescope. "We turned those perky teenagers against each other. But our work is not finished. Now that we have weakened the Power Rangers, we can get rid of them once and for all. Then the Earth will be mine to destroy. All mine!"

"Excuse me, Your Royal Evilness," said Finster.

"Don't interrupt me when I'm ranting!" screamed Rita.

Finster summoned up his courage and said, "It's only that I have created a new monster for you, Supreme Empress."

"A new monster! Why didn't you say so sooner, you dimwit? Show it to me immediately!"

After school, Jason, Trini, and Zack huddled outside the Angel Grove Youth Center. Jason pressed a button on the communicator he wore on his wrist and whispered, "Zordon, Billy and Kimberly are acting strange. We need your help."

"Yes. I know what's been going on," Zordon's deep voice replied. "I've been watching on my viewing globe. I will teleport you, Zack, and Trini to the command center. We need to make a plan. I will locate Kimberly and Billy and teleport them in a special force field."

As soon as the Power Rangers arrived at the secret command center, Zordon gave Alpha 5 his orders. The lights on the small robot's head blinked as he listened to the wizard, whose image floated in a column of green light.

"Bring Billy and Kimberly to the command center. Use the special isolation force field."

Alpha buzzed around the room, pressing buttons and pulling levers. A loud rumbling noise filled the command center. "Transporting now," said Alpha.

A huge plastic tube appeared in the middle of the room. Inside stood an angry Billy and Kimberly.

"What's going on, you little tin can?" growled Billy. He pressed both hands against the force field. "Let us out of this fish bowl, or when I get out of here, I'll use a can opener on your big tin head."

Kimberly sat cross-legged on the floor inside the circular force field. Since Zack, Jason, and Trini had seen her last, Kimberly had spray-painted her hair black.

"He will, too," she said, "and I'll help him. So let us out of here."

Zack looked at Zordon. "Can you clue us in here?"

"Yes, Zack," said Zordon. "Rita put a secret potion in Kimberly's Power Drink. When Billy and Kimberly drank it, it turned them *nasty.*"

"Is there any way to bring them back to normal?" asked Jason, eyeing Kimberly and Billy sadly.

"Yes," said Zordon. "There is a way. There is a special plant sap that contains the cure. It is the green sap of the singing squash plant. But it grows in a different universe."

"How do we get this singing squash plant?" asked Trini.

"I'm afraid you will not be able to get it," said Zordon. "We'll have to send Alpha 5."

"Aye-yi-yi-yi-yi!" said Alpha, spinning around the room. "Billy and Kimberly have gone punk and I have to go and get them a cure. Aye-yi-yi-yi-yi!"

Zack's dark eyes looked worried. "What if Alpha can't find the plant?"

"I am afraid," said Zordon, "that Billy and Kimberly will be lost forever to the forces of Evil."

CHAPTER 6

"Well, where is it?" Rita shouted at Finster. "I want to see this
new monster right now. And this
time I hope you did it right."

"I already sent it to Angel
Grove," said Finster. "But you can
see its picture." He opened his
book of monsters and showed

Rita his newest creation. It was the ugliest, bumpiest toad she'd ever seen, with a big horn on the top of its head—the Terror Toad!

"Oh, how cute!" said Rita. "I will keep it as a pet after it destroys the world for me."

"Uh, sure," said Finster. "But it's got a big appetite. And guess what it eats?"

"I hate guessing games!" cried Rita loudly. "What does it eat?"

"It eats teenagers—healthy, loud teenagers," Finster said. "And it just arrived in Angel Grove. Have a look."

Finster pressed the "on" switch to a large screen on the wall. It showed the Terror Toad on Main Street in Angel Grove. It was heading toward the mall!

"Eat teenagers," croaked the giant green monster. "Eat Power Rangers. Ha ha ha!"

When the toad laughed, its huge tongue fell out of its mouth and hit the ground. Its body shook all over.

"Now, I can destroy Earth and take over the universe," Rita screeched. "Not even Zordon can stop me!"

Back at Zordon's command center, Alpha 5 was getting ready to go in search of the only thing that could save Billy and

Kimberly. "But how will I know the plant?" Alpha asked Zordon.

"Don't worry," said Zordon. "You will hear the wonderful tones of the singing squash song."

Suddenly a loud buzzer sounded in the command center.

Trini jumped. "What's that?" she asked.

Zordon's voice boomed across the room. "That's the monster warning bell. It means Rita has sent a new monster to destroy the planet Earth. I can see it on the viewing globe. It's the Terror Toad!"

Jason leapt to his feet as he spotted the monster on the globe.

"We've got to stop it!" he gasped.

"Yes, Jason," said Zordon. "You, Zack, and Trini must return to Angel Grove to destroy this terrible toad. But be careful! This new monster's favorite food is teenagers. And without Billy and Kimberly to help, you're at a disadvantage. Take great care."

"No problem," said Zack.

"Okay guys, it's morphin time!" shouted Jason.

Trini, Zack, and Jason lifted their Power Morphers to the sky. Just as Zordon had taught them, they called upon the spirits of the ancient dinosaurs.

"Mastodon!" cried Zack.

"Saber-toothed Tiger!" cried Trini.

"Tyrannosaurus!" cried Jason.

In a flash, three ordinary teens from Angel Grove morphed into— Power Rangers!

Now they stood dressed as their super selves, in sleek uniforms and helmets. And with one more press of a button, they were on Main Street in Angel Grove.

"Let's kick some toad," said Zack. The three Power Rangers jogged forward to meet the Terror Toad in combat.

CHAPTER 7

"**Ready, Zack?**" asked Jason, the Red Ranger.

"Ready!" shouted the Black Ranger.

"Ready, Trini?" Jason turned to the Yellow Ranger.

"Ready!" replied Trini.

"Now remember," said Jason,

"this giant green geekoid eats teenagers. It's a lot more dangerous than it looks."

"Ugh," said Trini. "It has warts. I hope we don't have to touch it."

The ground shook as the toad hopped toward the Power Rangers. "Yum, yum, yum," it croaked. "Me hungry. Me want food. Ha ha ha!"

"Hit it!" Jason cried.

Zack twirled around and planted a solid kick in the toad's face. The Terror Toad just laughed, then knocked Zack into the air. Zack landed hard on the ground.

"Ki-yaaah!" Jason shouted as he landed two karate blows to the toad's body. But the Terror Toad didn't even blink.

Now it was Trini's turn. The Yellow Ranger streaked toward the toad, but before she could strike, it knocked Trini off her feet.

"Din-ner!" croaked the monster. A beam of light shot out of the toad's horn. The beam shone directly on Trini.

"Hey, what's going on?" yelled Trini. She tried to roll out of the beam, but she couldn't move. The beam grew brighter. Trini was being pulled forward into the gaping mouth of the Terror Toad!

In an instant, the monster swallowed her whole. Trini's face magically appeared on the Terror Toad's fat stomach, then she disappeared completely.

"No!" Zack shouted. He rushed toward the toad, but Jason held him back. "Let me go, man," Zack cried out. "I've got to help Trini."

"Wait a minute," said Jason. "We'll take this green bucket together. You attack from the right side and I'll nail it on the left."

Both Power Rangers raced to their positions, loaded their dart weapons, and aimed at the toad.

"Fire!" Jason shouted.

Their darts just bounced off the

monster's warty skin!

"Ha ha ha!" laughed the toad. Now the toad pointed its horn at Zack. "Din-ner!" Its magic beam sucked the Black Ranger right into its mouth.

"More food!" bellowed the Terror Toad, slowly starting toward Jason. Jason stood all alone.

CHAPTER 8

At the command center, Alpha had just returned with the singing squash. He quickly squeezed the green sap into two glasses of soda. Even the earplugs he wore didn't drown out the squash's shrieking.

"If this is what Zordon calls

'wonderful tones,' I'd hate to hear Zordon sing!" Alpha mumbled to himself as he worked.

The drinks fizzed and sparkled bright green. When they looked normal again, Alpha turned off the force field that held Kimberly and Billy and brought the drinks to them.

"Well, it's about time," said Kimberly. "I was wondering when that little buckethead was going to serve us something."

"Yeah," said Billy. "The service here stinks."

Kimberly and Billy grabbed the drinks and chugged them down. Instantly they started to shake.

Then they turned green. When they stopped trembling, they gazed around, confused. "Alpha? What's going on? What are we doing here?" they asked the robot.

Alpha 5 took off his earplugs and told Billy and Kimberly what had happened to them. He turned on the viewing globe to show them what was going on in Angel Grove.

"Jason really needs your help," said Zordon. "Listen carefully. My scanners tell me that there are two things you must do to kill the Terror Toad. First, you have to cut off its magic horn. Then you must hit its weakest spot—right under the chin."

"Got it," said Billy. "It's morphin time!"

The Power Rangers raised their Power Morphers into the air. They called on the powers of the ancient dinosaurs.

"Pterodactyl!" cried Kimberly.

"Triceratops!" cried Billy.

A crackling glow filled the command center.

"POWER RANGERS!" the two shouted as they morphed into the Blue and Pink Rangers. Then they teleported to Angel Grove—just as the Terror Toad caught Jason in its beam.

"Welcome back," Jason said as he struggled in the Terror Toad's force field. "This web-footed weirdo is one tough toad!"

Jason gasped as he was pulled forward, caught in the snarling toad's terrible tongue. And then he was gone.

The two Power Rangers cartwheeled out of the monster's reach, and blasted their weapons at its horn. Sparks flew as they sliced the horn right off.

"Ow, that hurts," croaked the toad.

"I'll distract it," Billy shouted to Kimberly. "Try for its weak spot!" Then the Blue Ranger rolled under the toad's bumpy body.

Kimberly aimed her bow and arrow at the monster's neck. As her arrows sailed through the air, the toad opened its ugly mouth and scooped up Billy with its slimy tongue!

Then Kimberly's sharp arrows struck—right on target! The toad's throat exploded into bits of green goo! Billy, Jason, Zack, and Trini were hurled from the toad's stomach unharmed.

"Hey, guys!" shouted Kimberly. "Are you okay?"

"Yeah," said Zack. "And I see you fried one bad toad!"

The five Power Rangers

slapped hands. They had saved the Earth from the forces of Evil. Rita Repulsa had lost again.

"Now we can finish our volleyball practice," Jason said to his friends.

"Great idea! Let's go," Trini agreed.

"Sure," said Zack. "On one condition. Billy and Kimberly, no more Power Drinks, okay?"

The Power Rangers laughed. "Let's go play some volleyball!"

Meanwhile, back in Rita's fortress on the moon, Rita clutched the sides of her head with her long, bony hands as she peered up at Earth. "Why can't I ever win?" she whined. "Why? Why? Why?" Then she laughed her evil laugh. "Just wait until next time, Power Rangers. And there will be a next time—soon!"